SURRENDER

DAILY ONE PEG IN THE MORNING KEEP'S EVERYTHING STEADY..

SESHU CHEERA

This book is dedicated to My Beloved Family, Lord Krishna, and My inspiration, Mr. Akella Raghavenda Rao guru. I don't have words to describe my family who has always stood by my side, even when I didn't.

Thank you to all my family members, friends and my well wishers..etc

Contents

FOREWORD

I've used all of the most well-known names in this hypothetical scenario. All of these people are entirely fictitious creations of mine. It is entirely coincidental if someone notices similarities in situations and characters. I hope you will abide by my request that you only treat them as fictitious characters.

Preface

My name is Seshu Cheera, and I was raised a Catholic. Lord Krishna was something I discovered. I am interested in Buddhist and Jain philosophy because I teach. I am not a religious person, but I do believe in God. I read both the Bible and the Bhagavad Gita. I like reading the Quran (if possible). In essence, I am a voracious reader. Among my favourite books are Secret, Power of the Subconscious Brain, 7 Habits of Highly Effective People, Zero to One, and others.

As a result, I realised that everything can be summed up in a single word: humanism. I consider myself a Humanist. I respect all Gods, Religions, and my fellow Humans.

This book is about parents' unwavering love for their children. Even when children are unaware, even when they understand, and even when they abandon them in pursuit of self-achievement. I'm not sure why people lose sight of the simple logic of "whatever they are today?" It is the result of a collaborative effort on the part of both parents.

I'm writing a character named Joseph who faces a few challenges in his life before overcoming them as he achieves some success in his career and becomes arrogant to his parents. However, because he is a devout Christian. He eventually realises what's going on. So the plot of this book is about how he acted before realising what he was doing and how he reacted after realising what he was doing.

When the new year began in January 2022, I made a vow to appreciate everyone for who they are, but after reading a few novels, I am unable to remain silent. As a result, I started jotting down my thoughts as they came to me. You may believe that your thoughts have tremendous

power. No, without a doubt.
I just want to talk to myself. This is unforgivable. As a result, I write solely for fun and to alleviate my loneliness.

I currently live in Hyderabad, Telangana, a southern state of India. I came here looking for work. I work as a teacher in one of Hyderabad's prestigious private schools.

This book is being written because I believe that many of us go through life believing that everything we do is perfect. Since 2008, several of my students have complained that their parents don't understand them. My mother, in particular, does not think highly of me. As a teacher, I used to persuade parents by emphasising the fact that children are sensitive and should be heard. I believed that children are righteous and sensitive. Is this correct? The majority of us believe I am correct. However, I was not one of them. I was speaking with a mother and father about their ward. It's hilarious to tell them they're sensitive.

Children, I've discovered, are sensitive, and they are the sole reason for parents to act. This is something I discovered after having a beautiful daughter in 2018. She is an angel in my life. This is the most precious gift that the Almighty Lord has given to me.

ACKNOWLEDGEMENTS

First and foremost, I want to thank Mother Mary for the numerous blessings she has bestowed upon my family.

I'd like to thank all of the priests who worked at Mary Matha Shrine in Gunadala, Vijayawada, Andhra Pradesh, India.

I'd also like to offer my heartfelt prayers to my teachers at St Joseph English Medium School. For many years, Mr. Johnson has been my math teacher and mentor. My principal, school correspondent, and all of my favourite teachers

Thank you to all of my classmates and friends for your unwavering support. My coworkers have all been teachers since 2008.

Above all, it was my students who accepted and believed that I was teaching them properly. From 2008 to the present day. I consider myself extremely fortunate to have been chosen as their teacher. My students are wonderful individuals, and I will miss them all when they leave for college. According to the Bible, children are to be regarded as a blessing rather than a hindrance. They are a divine recompense! Children truly are a gift from God.

Being a teacher is a true blessing. Thank you very much, Lord Almighty.

I

Chapter 1: Let's Begin

I was in an interview, and they were asking me questions, to which I responded to. The question of why you have so many fights emerged unexpectedly.

Yes, sir, I have differences with you because I don't respect those who don't respect me. This, I believe, is the foundation of human life philosophy.

But, sir, I was misinformed. This is something I've always believed in. As a result, I made a point of emphasizing my desire for respect. I will not respect you if you do not respect me. I'm not going to bother with respecting you.

I got a response confirming that I was correct. I said no... No, sir, I respectfully decline. Sir, you were mistaken.

I just learned that a priest died the day before yesterday.

I thought he was the source of a problem in my life. When I was 16, he was the one who tried to correct me. I was the least bothered. He blessed me, and now he is no longer with us.

I received a response, and everything is OK. You just had a

notion, didn't you? Yes or no is the answer.

Thank you, sir. But, sir, you were mistaken.

Means?

My family was initially impacted with a medical issue for my father when I was 16 years old. To call it an accident would be an understatement.

Before we get into the details, let me state unequivocally that my father is currently well and safe while this narrative is being written.

II

Introduction

Joseph is the name of the character. In 2017, Joseph married, and in 2018, he gave birth to a daughter. In India, he works as a teacher in the state of Karnataka. He is a teacher with strong morals. He is adamant that, along with his subject Math, the most important thing that children should learn is discipline.

Initially, Joseph worked in a nearby school. The Tripura Sundari Temple is roughly a one-and-a-half-hour drive from Agartala in the district town of Udaipur in Tripura. Joseph senior's grandparents used to have a deck overlooking one of the Brahmaputra River's tributaries.

Since I'm talking about the 1970s and 1980s, there aren't many rivers with bridges. As a result, every farmer requires a deck to transport their crops to a nearby town. Every farmer used to pay in produce rather than cash, thus my grandfather made a lot of money. So, while he is not a farmer, he has an equivalent supply of grains. My grant mother Sundari is the eldest of the three sisters, and my grandfather Joseph senior is the eldest of his five brothers.

I mean to emphasize that Joseph's family is quite large. After his parents died, my grandparents were left to care for the entire family.

Because he is the only boy, Joseph's father was given the name Paul. Paul is the second in line. He has two younger sisters and one older sister.

Paul is enrolled in a missionary school in the area. Because there is a lot of discrimination in our society,

He's a fantastic football player. He was named the top football player in his district, to be sure. He is a standout student at his school. As a result, he has a small number of female supporters.

Paul had evolved into a young guy with secondary features by the time he reached 10th grade. He began to attract the attention of females. He is a well-known football player at his high school.

It's sometime in the 1970s. Paul is the family's sole boy and the Joint family's first son.

He was raised with a great deal of respect and love.

He was smitten by Tripura, one of his classmates. She is exceptionally attractive and hails from a wealthy and powerful caste in Tripura.

This love tale lasted until 1978 when the family was tragically killed in a fire. Yes, someone set fire to Paul's house, and everything was destroyed. They were evicted from their home. The only saving grace is that no human lives were lost.

Paul's father is a Christ-follower. He thanked God that no human life had been lost. Then they were hired by the Tripura Sundari Temple. Senior Joseph accepted the contract to manage the temple's coconuts, head shaves, and hair sales, among other things.

The news of the fire accident went across the community.

Tripura's parents learned about Paul and his family as well. As a result, they took issue with Tripura's dealings with Paul. Paul is notified of the same.

My family is going through a crisis, Paul said, but it can be managed. However, I am unable to alter my social standing.

Tripura attempted to make her parents happy, but it all in vain.

She waited till she finished her studies before becoming a nun.

He had irrevocably lost her love. He made the decision to never love anyone again. Because it is excruciatingly unpleasant.

In 1981, Paul married Mary, the daughter of one of his sisters. He has two sons, one born in 1982 and the other in 1984. However, in 1984, he lost both of his parents. Paul now had to face the entire family's duty.

Paul's elder sister didn't want Paul to be the temple's heir to Joseph's contract.

Rose is her name, and she is a well-educated woman at the time. She holds a bachelor's degree. In the early 1980s, she used to be able to talk fluently in English. In 1983-84, she even travelled to Southeast Asian countries such as Singapore and Malaysia before her father died. As a result, she wishes to take responsibility for her family while also succeeding as the contract's successor, allowing her to continue handling her father's daily chores.

The temple priests opposed it, claiming that a woman couldn't perform it. They're fine if Mr. Paul is willing to take them. Paul is already married, and he and his wife have a son named Mario. At that point, Paul's wife is pregnant. A family member is also one of the qualifications, according to Mr. Bali, the chairman of the priests.

III

Internal Disputes

Rose had dedicated her life to this point, but she was troubled by the shifting circumstances when her father died. She fell into a deep depression. Examining the circumstance.

Paul is obliged to shoulder all of the family's responsibilities, and he is forced to forsake his dream profession of traveling abroad as his sister did. He is a graduate and a well-known football player in the district. But, as it is the Time, he must stand up for his family and fulfill his obligations.

As a superb football player, Paul is constantly responsible, disciplined, and committed. As Swami Vivekananda correctly stated, this made him physically and intellectually powerful.

Paul began by getting up at 4 a.m. to wash the Mother Goddess's shrine and prepare everything for the Priest's daily prayers; afterward, he managed employees for coconut collecting and maintained workers for a head shave and hair collection once it was shaved. He used to work and collect commissions as a way to supplement his children's income. Paul is blessed with another Boy Baby the next year. As a tribute to his father, he called his second son Joseph.

He is blessed with another Boy baby two years later. Mary was furious with her third son because she was anticipating a girl baby at least for the time being. As a result, Paul's family is now complete.

Paul has become more focused and dedicated to his work, while Rose has improved and married a jack. They are the proud parents of a little girl. They afterwards relocated to another country. Sundari, their mother, died the same year.

IV

Rising of Joseph

Paul is the shrine's most important member. With his effort, he steadily improved and gained respect for Mother Goddess Tripura Sundari. He was raised as a Catholic, yet he sees Goddess Tripura Sundari as Jesus Christ's Mother Mary. Mother is Mother wherever she is. He began to pray for both of them equally.

Mary desired that Paul educate our children in English. He is thrilled, but he is beginning to wonder if he will be able to afford such high costs. However, he assured her that they would do something for their children.

Mary is a stunning and attractive woman. That is why she taught Paul that if she only had one daughter, he would not mourn his mother. She enjoys her mother-in-law and grandmother as well.

Now that both Paul and Mary have elected to educate their children at a catholic school, a Temple-associated school is a conventional local language school, as only Christian schools at the time were English medium.

Paul notified the temple priest and sought his guidance on the schooling of the children.

Mr. Bali, the priest, summoned him to his office and thanked him for his suggestion. He also looked at their horoscopes.

He advised Paul that, according to his birth chart, Joseph requires special attention and that, when he approaches the age of 16, he may have some challenges. He'll also have to deal with a slew of issues. You must remain awake and observant at all times. I'm sharing this with you solely to remind you to stay awake and focused on your work. As I may not be permanently here. If you desire, I will take care of your family wherever I go. You don't have to think twice, Paul; I consider your wife to be my own daughter. Then Paul told him that his wife, Mary, had an ambition of teaching all of her children in English.

Paul smiled warmly and said, I'm fine if I die doing my duty to my family. I don't believe all of these birth charts, but Mr. Bali, you have my respect. Thank you so much for your time and consideration. I'm taking on my father's responsibilities. So, until they allow me to serve, I'd rather serve Mother Goddess Tripura Sundari. I can't stop if something is written for me to read, and neither can you. Is that correct, sir? Yes, Paul, you are truly a blessed soul.

Mr. Bali, a Hindu Monk, aided Paul and his family by donating a quarter to their cause.

As a result, Paul and his family became a talking point. They are given a quarter to dwell in the Hindu temple grounds because they are Christians.

Paul told his wife about his conversation with Mr. Bali. She expressed her gratitude by saying, "I feel truly blessed to have my name associated with both of you." Mary was warned by Paul to be on the lookout for Joseph. As he gets older, he can have some difficulties.

Joseph, along with his brothers Sundar and Mario, enrolled

at the school. The priests and monks also backed Paul up whenever he needed it.

Every four years, the monks would change. Mr. Ram assumed control of the temple once Mr. Bali was transferred. Mr. Ram used to be friendly with Paul because they were the same age, and he gave assistance to him by extending the contract. Joseph is now in the eighth grade. He aspired to become a Christian Priest. Paul agreed to marry Joseph but asked Mary to persuade him to abandon his plans to leave me. As you know, I chose his name in honor of my father. By the time he reaches the age of 16, he will have gone through some difficult periods as well.

I can't afford anything like that. I can't say no to him since I consider him to be my father.

Is he gone? How did his mother make his life easier for him?

V

Sweet 16 circle

Priesthood attempt: When Joseph was in his early teens, he began to believe that he was aware of a lot of things.
As a monk in the shrine, Joseph enjoys being revered. As a result, he desired to be regarded, despite his limited understanding. He thought that if we become monks, I would be revered and wouldn't have to work as much as his father Paul. Joseph used to admire his father and would proudly proclaim that his father not only works as a barber but also as a contractor. As a result, he was shunned by a handful of his pals.

When he was six years old, he inquired as to why his mother and father were both unemployed. A couple of my friends' fathers work as teachers, drivers, and inspectors, for example.
Yes, your father works as a barber for a living, Joseph's mother said. He's doing it because we're the ones who have to do it. He is free to do whatever he wants.

Is there anything else he can do than work as a barber? In the 7th Garde, he is a district foot player awardee. He outplays everyone else in the district when it comes to football.

He truly understands football. Yes, if you have any doubts, please consult your physical education teacher.

Why is he going to say that?

Because your father, Paul, and Peter, are best friends and classmates.

Oh, can dad be a sports teacher, a football coach, etc., Joseph asked.

He is a graduate, Mother replied. So, why is he performing this kind of pointless work?

Isn't that all he's doing? He's just doing what your grandfather taught him to do?

What did my grandfather say to my father?

Take care of his family and my children, Mother replied. Continue to serve Mother Goddess as best you can. That is the most important work for us; I have made a lot of money in my life, but I have never been as happy as we are today. "You will be blessed, my son, and I will be proud of you."

Okay, now I understand that the most important thing I can do on this planet is to serve God in any way I can.

As a result, he chose to become a priest.

Failed Priest Hood attempt: At the age of 13, Joseph opted to pursue Priest Hood training, but due to a lack of facilities, such as the requirement that every trainee priest wash their own clothes, he was unable to complete the program. As a result, Joseph's mother objected to such methods and stated that they were unnecessary. Joseph was disappointed, but Paul feels relieved since Joseph will be with him.

As a house leader, Joseph grew up to be a very diligent and disciplined young man. From 1999-to 2000, he was nominated as one of the Four Houses Leaders. He was in Grade X at the time.

He received 76 percent in grade X and desired to pursue a profession as a software developer. Because he began to hear on the news that the Y2K problem is becoming more prevalent, and that computer professionals will be able to earn a lot of money in the future. From 1999-to 2000, he learned MS Office, Java, and Oracle7.3. When Joseph applied for admission, he overheard his father conversing with the director of the computer training facility. He was unable to complete the course due to a gap in Grade X Board exams. When he returned to tutoring after the exams, he discovered that the institute had been sold to the new administration.

Paul made an attempt, but his efforts were in vain. Joseph felt guilty as well but intended to pursue engineering and eventually become a software engineer.

After starting college in 2000-2002, he majored in Math, Physics, and Chemistry with the goal of getting into engineering school.

Joseph had completed his final year examinations and was looking forward to his summer vacation. Paul was not feeling good because he is suffering from Malaria.

As a result, he was brought to the hospital and treated. He began to feel better.

Paul was sweating profusely at exactly 8 p.m. Joseph ran to the doctor and informed him of the situation. The doctor immediately advised him to go to the emergency room. Everything was turned on its head. He was placed on a ventilator and doctors recommended he notify his entire family.

Due to a few alterations in the contract between Paul and Shrine changed by the Monks, Joseph's family's financial condition gradually began to deteriorate.

People have begun to notice the increase in Paul's family's income and social status, such as his children attending an English medium school on par with the society's higher caste dominant members. As a result, it became unavoidable for the monks to exert some control over Paul's contract and financial flow.

As a result of such thinking in society, monks decided to take up the tasks that Paul and his family had been doing for the past two decades. They agreed to organize a monastic committee to research other approaches and form a commission of monks to study them.

Following a series of negotiations, it was agreed to cancel the contract and hire staff to manage the activities and report directly to the shrine's in-charge Monk.

The majority of the monks have agreed to this.

VI

Twist and Turns

As a result of this information, Paul was informed of the Shrine's change of mind regarding the Contract and its terms and conditions.

Unaware of this, Paul's wife planned to build a house on a parcel of land that the family had inherited. She had set aside some funds and decided to construct a home. In the next three months, she planned and built a house. She is a devout Christian who, at the age of 28, chose to create a home. Even the most educated among us may not consider building our own home right now.

Paul was first dissatisfied with the decision because he was aware that a few modifications to his contract and work status were on the way. He was concerned and didn't want to tell his wife anything. Let's wait a month, he said. She adores him and is completely devoted to him. She said, "OK," but asked if everything was fine. You appear to be unsettled these days. He stated that he has been receiving signals about a modification in the contract's terms and circumstances and that the monks have been holding a series of meetings for the past month.

"Don't worry, sweetie, about anything; if they don't want to keep us, we'll look for other work," she said. You're not just working for monks and contracts; you're also serving Mother Goddess, and she'll look after us." I believe her, but you are skeptical.

However, adjusting from working as a contractor to working solely as one of the company's employees was not easy. He had previously worked.

VII

Disturbance of emotions

What has changed?

He receives a 30% commission on the ticket price. For example, if a head-shaving ticket costs Rs. 10/-, Paul receives Rs. 3/- each ticket. As part of the contract, he must keep the personnel to serve the people. He used to work as an employee out of ten employees whom he used to appoint to complete the duties as per the contract because he has a family.

He used to get a daily commission at the end of the day, which he would pay out to his coworkers and use to feed his family.

As a result, he was able to supplement his income while still continuing to serve Mother Goddess as promised to his late father Joseph at the time of his death.

Now that the contract has been voided, Monk has stated that he would continue to work for the temple and will be paid a wage rather than a commission.

It is nearly impossible for anyone to accept his

predicament. Paul began to accept things as they are. Paul just believed that his life was now encircled by problems. He began to drink alcohol on a daily basis. He used to work with his coworkers as he had in the past.

But Mary didn't find out until he lapsed into a coma in May 2002.

My father was sick:

Paul was admitted to the hospital with malaria fever, but he was being treated. However, despite the fact that he had only a few injections, he experienced a reaction during his treatment. He was having a lot of reactions since he was diabetic. However, the family is ignorant of this.

As a result, he has been having high blood sugar levels, which has rendered him comatose for a few hours. He gets admitted to the hospital right away.

Mr. Bhanu and his team of doctors are in charge of transferring him to the emergency ward.

He was able to recuperate after 24 hours. He has been advised to take a few months off. The entire family was overjoyed.

Joseph has been tasked with paying the medical bills.

Insufficient funds:

Now Joseph returned to his home and attempted to collect money from a number of locals. He is also urging that every money lender near the shrine contribute a sum of Rs 50000/-. He also requested that house paperwork be held and given, totaling 3 lakhs.

Because his mother also donated all of her gold ornaments and made the initial payment.

No one has expressed a desire to lend money to Joseph's family. While Joseph returns with a feeling of rejection in his heart. His thoughts are now filled with dread about his father's medical expenditures.

"Are you there?" he exclaimed as he turned back to Mother Goddess Shrine. Are you genuine? My father has been serving you for the past 16 years? If this is the case.

Why isn't anyone assisting me? Why aren't you seeing everything? Please, if you're there, take action.

Tears stream down his cheeks and out of his eyes.

He arrived at his Grandparents' house and was greeted by his mother.

"What happened?" she inquired.

Mother, Joseph said, "It's no use." I attempted to contact all of the money lenders. They resisted me. I was asked, "How will you pay?" You have no idea what you're talking about. Even your mum does not work.

She inquired as to what had happened to Gold. Mother, I sold it; do we need a bit extra cash?

Joseph sobbed and remarked, "I never knew that people were valued just because of my father, not for their money, wealth, or possessions." I make a wish to the goddess Mother. I don't want him to be in such a financial bind.

Joseph's favorite person is his grandmother. He bears a striking resemblance to her in terms of skin tone, demeanor, and values.

She had come to inquire about the financial arrangements. Joseph responded, "No."

Don't worry, she added, let's pray to God. There will be action taken.

They all slept and prayed.

On that particular morning, Joseph's mother, Mary, was in a terrible mood. Joseph observed it and questioned, "Mother, are you planning for the rest of your expenses?"

No, I'm concerned about Joseph. Your Uncle is prepared to make the necessary financial arrangements. But who will assist us for a few months until your father recovers to his full potential?

David, your uncle, is a government official and Mary's brother. She said you just finished your Higher Secondary exams, but will you be able to drop out of school and work to help support our family? I'm also considering going to work.

I will undoubtedly become a mother, and I am unconcerned about my education. I'll do everything I can to assist my father in regaining his health as quickly as possible.

As a result, she requested that he seek assistance from Uncle David.

David entered the house and asked if you wanted to work in the hotel industry because you speak English well.

He claimed I had no idea "how to do any work?"

I know a school where you can study, and we'll get you in. Joseph felt it was my responsibility to assist my family at this time.

Mary was dissatisfied because it appeared that additional money would be required.

Joseph consented and agreed to work despite the fact that he was unaware of it.

David and Joseph both proceeded to find out more information.

They returned after two hours.

When he entered the house, he noticed his Father lying in bed, his face beaming with joy.

At home, everyone was content.

After a while, Joseph continued to complain about his lack of funds.

His mother replied, her gaze fixed on his. By gazing at his expression, she comprehended the query. She is the mother of three.

Yes! Dear, your prayer has been answered. The shrine monk arrived and paid off all of the bills. Shrine has also vowed to support him until he gets back to normal. They also expressed regret for the delay in their response.

Joseph was overjoyed and expressed his gratitude to Mother Goddess for her blessings.

Taking on the responsibility:

Now that Joseph is more relaxed, he has attempted to attend a couple hotel interviews:

He went to the first one and failed since he didn't know what he was doing. He informed his mom as well.

She asked if you could think of something else to do instead of working in the hotel industry. That industry does not appeal to me.

He persisted on going nicely dressed and taking a steward job, oblivious to her comprehension. He persuaded his uncle David to put up Rs 10,000.

VIII
Fell down & Failed

But you won't be able to do it, Joseph. We are not obligated to undertake only this type of work. Try something different.
She has taken Joseph under her wing. She understands that he is unable to receive directions in front of others. He isn't used to giving suitable responses. He has a strong sense of self-confidence. He only wears white sandals.
She is attempting to make him aware of a crisis situation that will need to be dealt with in the near future.
Joseph says yes, but he has no idea what is about to happen? He will get himself into difficulty unnecessarily.

After 15 days, he began to notice people's true attitudes. He is unable to move for long periods of time in the early morning due to his affiliation with one hotel. In the hotel, he was unable to serve the guests.
Everything is being noticed by his mother. His grandma chastised him for his failure to fit into jobs one day. He has squandered money in an unnecessary manner.

He overheard it and became upset. Because he adores her. Mary forewarned Joseph because she was aware of the circumstance.

The situation deteriorated. Mary insisted on returning to our own residence near the shrine since she had no other choice. Joseph is now scared because his mother lived like a queen, with a large number of servants working for his father.

She never left the house unless it was absolutely necessary. She used to go to church with him on a daily basis.

Our financial situation has deteriorated recently. He began to disguise his nervousness and push back against her remarks.

But he loves her so much that he couldn't stand up to his mother's efforts.

Mary is also concerned that his family may suffer as a result of the issue. She made the decision to work. Instead of relying on her own family, she prepared to work in the temple, cleaning and serving Mother Goddess.

Joseph is concerned about his mother's well-being and does not want her to suffer any difficulties if she returns to our home. They are no longer respectful of us.

Joseph based his viewpoint on a single experience. People questioned him because he observed their attitudes? What are your options?

Mary wishes to assist her husband and children. She, on the other hand, does not want to be with her own family, which is slightly wealthier than her husband's. Her father works for the railways, and her brother is a government teacher. They're even pleading with her to abandon her husband and children and join them.

As a result, she decides to remain with her spouse. Yes, Paul is now suffering from a health problem. Today he appears to be frail.

That is correct. I'd like to spend all of my time with him. In our shrine, I heard Bhagavad Gita and Ramayana several times. I'll return and do everything I can to keep my spouse and family happy.

Joseph and even Mary's mother, Rose, were taken aback by her reaction and decision to return to her home as quickly as possible. She is unable to maintain herself due to a lack of funds. Even Joseph is taken aback by her choice to leave her home and travel to a location where her father worked.

He adores his mother because he witnessed her genuine affection for his father. So he said this time, "We'll go back." I swear to you all. My mother does not have to work as long as I am alive. Thank you for your help during this difficult time.

Rose gave him a hug and replied, "OK." I have faith in you. You were all born in a temple. You will be helped by God. I'll do my part as well. She sobbed as she caught Mary and apologized, saying, "I didn't mean any harm to you."

Your grandmother wishes to speak with you.

Then you're free to go. When Mary visited her grandparents, she insisted on taking a present even though she didn't think it was necessary.

She is free to return it whenever she wishes. However, for the time being, please take.

Mary took out the loan with the promise of repaying it. At the age of 28, she returned to her home and built her own house. She returned, and Joseph trailed behind her. Paul is on the mend and is able to return to work. He told the shrine that he might be able to return to work as a daily wage laborer. Daily wage workers are paid Rs 50/- every day.

Now Joseph faces a new challenge: ensuring that his younger brother, who is in Grade X, continues his schooling.

Joseph must take a break for his studies, but the younger child must finish his basic schooling.

As a result, Joseph began working in a grocery. Paul Joseph's father, too, recovered and returned to work.

The family is now back to normal, but they do not have a steady source of money to support them. Joseph approached his class instructor, who also happened to be his math teacher, about his brother's education. He approached the management and arranged for his brother's schooling to be completed.

IX

Support

Brother's role: During times of stress, he is an unseen pillar of strength for me. He spent his adolescence solely concerned with how to keep the situation stable and complete his schooling.

From Grade X to Post-Graduation, he encountered a lot of discrimination at his educational institutions because they were not financially stable. He used to put forth a great deal of effort and apply for scholarships. Even though he has been surrounded by so many mental, social, and emotional disturbances since his adolescence, he is so dedicated to his studies.

He channelled his suffering or grief into studies, receiving a master's degree with honours and passing the state level lecturership exam. This demonstrates his resolve to pursue higher goals by channelling his misery into success. The logic is simple: we can do anything by overcoming obstacles and channelling our energy. The bigger the difficulty we face, the greater our opportunity to grow. The trials should strengthen you rather than weaken you. He is presently employed by the state government.

Many people in his hometown now look up to him as an inspiration.

Father is on the path to recovery:

Paul began to recover as the months passed, and things began to fall into place. Joseph now works as a courier boy to help support his family. Joseph was unhappy because he noticed that only a few of his classmates were going into Engineering.

As he wants to pursue a career in computer engineering, the situation appears to be nearly impossible. So Joseph wept and begged his mother, "Why is my life going this way?" Should I be like this for the rest of my life? Is there anything we can do?

Both felt awful, and Joseph's mother, Mary, said, "It never occurs according to our will." It is the Almighty God's will. It isn't the end of the world if you can't study anymore. Allow your father to heal, and we'll see what we can do to get you enrolled in any university graduating.

I believe you can pray to God and express your desire to study. Make a prayer to Mother Mary. You have the option of studying something. It's possible that we won't be able to finish the engineering.

As a result, Joseph felt irritated for a few days. After 6 months, he enrolled in an art graduate programme at one of Assam's top universities. He maintained his studies while also working part-time to help support his family with his little earnings.

He continued his education after graduation, passing the UGC-NET, a national eligibility test for lecturership, in a single session in 2008. This instilled confidence in him, and he went on to work as a teacher in a local Christian school. He was employed there for five years. Later, in order to improve his prospects and income, he relocated to Noida to work for an international school. He was invited to one of his friend's parties one day. Marriage between classmates. In the year 2008, He ran into all of his friends. As a result, he was standing in a corner. His first love surprised him by showing up with her mother and introducing Joseph to her, adding, "He is a wonderful person." He appeals to me. He did an excellent job.

Joseph was taken aback because she used to ignore him at school. He has never had such high regard.

But when she mentioned him, it was a different story. He inquired as to what she was up to. She stated that she is employed at JNU as an Assistant Professor. Wow! It's wonderful to hear this. "No, Joseph," she said. "You are superior to all of us."

Really?

Yes, you defended your family when it was necessary. You didn't read the Ramayana, yet you acted like Rama. However, many people may not see this as significant. You're a true inspiration.

Joseph is ecstatic. When he liked her, he was ignored. She now describes me as an inspiration.

He told his mom Mary about it. She stated that you are unaware of the Ramayana plot; I agree, yet I am proud of you, my son.

Slowly, both of their phone numbers were swapped, and they fell in love all over again. But now that Joseph and Sowjanya are adults, they both work as teachers. They realized that their families' caste and economic position were in the east and west directions. As a result, they decided not to go any further.

Both agreed and left, as Joseph's feat was not particularly noteworthy. Joseph is now concentrating on accumulating some wealth for his family in order to keep his father and mother happy.

In 2014, he relocated to the NCR region, which includes Delhi and Noida. He taught in a number of prestigious international schools. He was unable to adapt to the culture of the traditional schools. He learned how to make a good living and support his family for the following five years. He began to develop arrogance as a result of his high salary. He began to ignore his parents' advise to save money for future needs.

He began to spend money on high-priced foods, things, and products.

X

Changed Scenario

Mary isn't fond of his demeanor. She sent the same message to him. Joseph dismissed her suggestion, stating, "I have accomplished something today, and I have every right to spend money as I prefer mum." At the age of 16, I was afflicted. At the age of 29, I'm having a good time. Is it impossible for me to do that right now?

Mary expressed her regret. I had no intention of hurting you.

She was hurt by Joseph's statements, and she had the impression that he was becoming more interested in material things. She understands that Joseph is sensitive and that if he is injured again, he would be upset. However, Joseph is oblivious to the fact that everything is a phase.

It goes through a declining and waxing phase. During both phases, we must learn to be stable. He isn't ready to listen and comprehend this life philosophy. Mary made the decision to pray for Joseph. The benefit of the child, not the materials, money, or position, is always at the forefront of a mother's mind.

According to Joseph, these are his accomplishments. He was able to make a comfortable living. He never anticipated he would be able to earn $40,000 when he began working at the age of 16 to support his family in 2002.

With a master's degree in political science and then a bachelor's degree in teaching, he worked and managed to support his family as well as his education. He began teaching in 2008 and has subsequently moved to an international school. He began to see life in a new light as well.

Marriage is a great celebration and a major occasion in the lives of every young person in India.

Joseph was looking for a simple girl who cared about her ideals rather than her possessions. Joseph's parents chose to look for a lady between the ages of 25 and 30 because he is now 33. After a lot of difficulties, they eventually found him a match in the form of a girl named Rosy, who is 28 years old and a postgraduate.

In November 2017, they married as a result of this. Following some initial problems in the marriage relationship, In 2018, Joseph was gifted with a Beautiful Girl baby, which he named Princess Diana.

Joseph is now living in the middle class, tailoring his income to his family's and parents' needs. He is unable to meet the needs of his family and his mother-in-family laws in many ways.

Joseph, who has been a devout Catholic from childhood and a firm believer in God, realized that his life was not going as planned. His wage is insufficient, especially after marriage.

He considered relocating his workplace. However, guess what? It didn't work. His pay was increased.

His life was flipped upside down when he was placed on lockdown for 18 months due to a global pandemic. As a teacher, he has battled to make ends meet throughout the economic downturn. The education sector has been hit the worst. Parents adore their children and bear as much as they can with their activities, but the world will never spare anyone. This is the outcome Joseph's mother foresaw.

Joseph began to work on himself at this point. He is a voracious reader. He began reading books with Robin Sharma's The Monk Who Sold His Ferrari, then Secret, Power of Positive Thinking, and Power of Subconscious Brain. As a man considers.

He developed a passion for reading. Things started to look odd around him. He began to see how he was limiting himself. In his mind, there is a stumbling barrier.

He began to concentrate more intently on his personal growth. Every day, he began to listen to a book summary and jot down the main elements. Over the course of a month, he developed into a confident speaker and a motivational instructor at his school.

He has the ability to deduce the causes of his failures. He gathered all of his memories and examined his demeanour. "Knowing oneself is the beginning of all wisdom," he discovered. As Aristotle once stated.

XI

I fell in love once more.

Joseph began to improve himself. He first completed a ten-things assignment to learn about his likes, dislikes, dreams, possessions, failures, and so on.

He began to consider what the meaning of life was. He began to listen to Lord Krishna's Bhagavad Gita as part of his daily regimen.

It teaches renunciation and duty action. Knowledge, action, and love are the three major themes. It provides you with a distinct way of life and allows you to live a happy, tension-free life. It is also a life scripture, in addition to being religious text. He was enamored with Lord Krishna's delivery of the notion and became a devout follower of Lord Krishna and his teachings.

He realized that the Almighty God is one and the same. "Jnana is the awareness of a man's inherent divinity via knowledge," Vivekananda said. It teaches man that he is, at his core, divine. The doctrine of the Trinity defines God as one God manifested in three divine Persons, even in

Christianity (each of the three Persons is God himself). God the Father, God the Son (Jesus), and God the Holy Spirit make up the Most Holy Trinity.

Joseph began to realize that there is only one God. To contact God, you can follow any religion of your choice. You can call him whatever you like, but there is only one God—Bhagavan, Almighty, and so on.

He discovered that his issues stemmed from a lack of life awareness and restrictive ideas.

We all have self-imposed limitations. We are constantly attempting to select or pick certain concepts from the environment that we believe are correct. We also choose from a variety of theories, stories, concepts, and quotes.

It's the same as when we're driving down the road and have to stop for spread brakes, traffic signals, turns, and other things. Similarly, we shape ourselves by believing that our thoughts, values, and beliefs are our strengths and attempting to adhere to them. With those thoughts and belief-based actions, we can sometimes accomplish success.

Is there a problem with that? No.

Please proceed to believe it if you are capable of achieving success in our lives. I mean, success entails making and assisting all of your loved ones, as well as our own satisfaction.

If you or anybody else in your immediate vicinity is unhappy. Whether it's in terms of money, emotions, or spirituality. Then it's time for you to reconsider your position. I began to reconsider... I resigned from my teaching position. This decision had a huge and unexpected impact on my life. Joseph is now unemployed. He wants to do something that will make him happy and prosperous in life. People, including relatives and friends, chastised, advised, and suggested him.

XII

Re-start

"He can accomplish much better in life," Joseph believes. As a result, he begged his entire family to grant him some time to unwind and restart his life. He took a breather...

I'd be delighted to tell you about his accomplishments. In the following surrender series.

The story seemed to come to an abrupt conclusion. Please put an end to it. It's just a twist of fate in Joseph's life.

Every person should do a self-evaluation, analyze, and interpret his or her life in order to make it a successful narrative. Why?

Because we only have one life to live. Any ambitions to achieve anything in life can and should be realized. I developed a list of a few thoughts that guided Joseph to be confident based on my observations.

First, believe in yourself. Believe that you can perform the work, start a business, or do whatever it is that you want to do. You possess all of the necessary abilities. It's possible that you won't be able to complete it in one go. When you're down, realise that there's always another chance, and give it your all to try again with a different strategy. Never allow

yourself to believe that you have no chance of winning.
At least three chances, I feel, can be tried.
Second, take control of your life. Today, we live in a world full of possibilities. You'll find them if you keep looking.
Third, be a self-loving person. You are exactly who you think you are. Don't attempt to be someone else's idea of a decent person.For you and them, the world is different.
After a few years, the same people will refer to your tale as an example to others.
Four, make it a habit to read. The greatest method to exercise your brain is to read a few books that work as a brain gym and encourage you to do things that are out of the norm.
Five: Always remember that we all have a war going on inside of us. To begin, work on overcoming your inner fears. You can see your own potential and vitality.
Sixth, tears allow you to let go of your inner stress. Once you've been pain-free for a while. You'll be able to regain your strength. It's inevitable that you'll become emotional. Never try to control your emotions; instead, learn to be with them. It has the potential to be harmful to one's health.

You can't open up to anyone if you can't open up to yourself. When you're going through an emotional whirlwind, try to be alone.
Seventh, never believe you're alone. If you make earnest efforts to accomplish something, the universe will back you up. It's true. That is correct.
Eighth, life is more than you can imagine. The majority of our problems or concerns stem from our ability to imagine the worst-case scenario. If anything truly tragic occurs, you must remain awake and face it. The more steady you are in a certain scenario, the better. You'll be able to handle it without difficulty. Whatever is happening, there is a reason

for it.

Acquire the ability to be versatile and flexible. People immediately rushed to the conclusion that they rely on god or nature for everything. It isn't entirely accurate, but it may reflect some people's experiences. However, you should never make a decision based on emotion. What do you think is the best option based on your knowledge? Never try to hurt someone else with your words, acts, or deeds.

Nine: Keep going. Never do anything that jeopardizes your self-respect or integrity. You'll know you're doing the right thing if only to yourself. I'm not talking about office jobs and responsibilities. Simply live a happy and ever-present existence. You are the only one who can make the decision. There is no one else.

ten: Take action toward your goal on a daily basis. Do everything in little steps and you'll be able to achieve your objective in no time. But do it every day in the morning, without fail. My favourite habit is to read or listen to at least one book summary per day.

Conclusion: I would like to encourage you to give your ego to the Almighty and focus on achieving a little bit better today than yesterday. Each of us has only one human life. Don't let a tiny previous event or the stories of a loved one limit your life. I agree that what you said is truthful, inspiring, and encouraging. Simply make yours someone else's inspiration. Thank you very much.

XIII

Final word

The tagline "Daily a small peg in the morning, keeps things stable" is probably what most of you are thinking of. I mean, if you spend 15-30 minutes each morning working on a talent you want to improve or obtain, you will get better as the days pass. In this sentence, I just used the peg to draw people's attention; I'm referring to a daily dose of improvement. To recuperate from disease, doctors recommend taking a daily dose. In the same way, I encourage everyone to improve on a daily basis; we can enhance anything we desire by practising it every day. You could also take pleasure in your life as a lifelong learner.

Good luck with your efforts...

Continue to smile...

I'm going to sign off...

Greetings, Seshu!

9 798886 672770

Printed by Libri Plureos GmbH in Hamburg,
Germany